Little Red Robin

Silly Name for a Monster

Do you have all the Little Red Robin books?

- ☐ Buster's Big Surprise
- ☐ The Purple Butterfly
- ☐ How Bobby Got His Pet
- ☐ We are Super!
- ☐ New Friends
- ☐ Robo-Robbie
- ☐ The Fleas Who Fight Crime
- ☐ A Friend for Dragon
- ☐ When the Tooth Fairy Forgot

Silly Name for a Monster

Little Red Robin

Timothy Knapman
Illustrated by Steve May

SCHOLASTIC

To Mimi and Jonathan, who have
wonderful names, with love T.K.

Scholastic Children's Books
An imprint of Scholastic Ltd.
Euston House, 24 Eversholt Street
London, NW1 1DB, UK
Registered office: Westfield Road, Southam, Warwickshire, CV47 0RA
SCHOLASTIC and associated logos are trademarks and/or registered
trademarks of Scholastic Inc.

First published in 2014 by Scholastic Ltd

Text copyright © Timothy Knapman, 2014
Illustrations © Steve May, 2014

The rights of Timothy Knapman and Steve May
to be identified as the author and illustrator of
this work have been asserted by them.

ISBN 978 1407 14408 5

A CIP catalogue record for this book is available from the British Library.

Printed in China.

1 3 5 7 9 10 8 6 4 2

www.scholastic.co.uk

Chapter One

Once upon a time, names were very important. You couldn't be a butcher if your name was Baker or a baker if your name was Butcher. It was against the law.

It was the same for heroes. To be a hero, you had to have a proper hero-type name. And if you were a big scary monster, your name had to be big and scary too.

Imagine being a monster, stomping around scaring people. You might be as big as a castle. You might be able to breathe fire from your earholes. But if your name was *Miss Mimsey Lovely-Pants*, you wouldn't be able to eat people. Why not? Because they'd be laughing too much.

It wasn't nice and it wasn't fair, but that was how things were.

Once there was a massive and menacing
Monster. It was huge and fierce and frightening.
It had horns and jaws and spikes and claws and
armpits that smelt like very old cheese.

This Monster was prowling and growling around. It was looking for somebody to scare when it came to a castle. It peered in at one of the windows.

There was the King, having a bath.

"Boo!" said the Monster.

"Eek!" shrieked the King, he jumped out of the bath and ran away.

Then he sneaked back in, grabbed his rubber duck and ran away again.

The King ran straight to the Royal Hero's room. It was the Royal Hero's job to fight all the King's enemies. He was tall and strong and handsome, and he had a proper hero-type name: *Sir Desmond the Daring.*

"A massive and menacing Monster just said 'Boo!' to me in the bath!" said the King.

"Poor you," said Sir Desmond. 'Would you like a towel, your Majesty?"

(The King had run off so quickly that he had forgotten to put any clothes on.)

"Ooh, yes! Thank you," said the King. "I thought it was a bit chilly in here. Anyway. There's a Monster out there. It's huge and fierce and frightening."

"Well, I hope you're not expecting *me* to do anything about it," said Sir Desmond. "I might get my armour scratched."

Sir Desmond thought looking smart was very important. He didn't like doing brave things because he hated getting stains on his chain mail.

"What am I going to do?" asked the King.

And then he had a brilliant idea.

That afternoon, everyone gathered in the castle courtyard. The King was going to make an important speech. The Royal Trumpeters blew their royal trumpets.

"The brave hero who can save us from this massive and menacing Monster shall have half my kingdom as a reward!" said the King.

"Hooray!" cried everyone. "We're saved!"

The kingdom was full of brave heroes with
proper hero-type names.

There was Sir
Richard the Brave,

Sir Geoffrey
the Fearless

and Sir Keith the
Stark Raving Bonkers.

One of them was bound to defeat the Monster.

Without delay, they set off on their proper hero-type horses: Greased Lightning, Thunder Hooves, GG-1000.

Swinging their proper hero-type weapons: The Goblin Grinder, The Dragon Damager, The Mighty Minotaur Mallet.

They never came back.

They took one look at the massive and menacing Monster and decided they didn't fancy being heroes after all.

They'd much rather spend the rest of their lives dancing around in pink frilly knickers.

"This is terrible!" cried the King.

"Terrible? It's a disaster!" said Sir Desmond, who was looking at himself in the mirror. "This new suit of armour makes my bottom look fat!"

"I meant: who is going to get rid of the Monster?" said the King.

"Oh, all right then," said Sir Desmond. '*I'll* go. But I'll need a *proper* reward. My suit of armour is bound to get *ruined*!"

So the next morning, the King made another important speech:

"The brave hero who can save us from this massive and menacing Monster shall have ALL my kingdom as a reward!"

"I shall do it, sire!" cried Sir Desmond.

"Hooray!" said everybody in the crowd. Well, everybody but one.

"Boo!" said a small cross-looking boy. "Why does he get to be the Royal Hero?'

"Because I am tall and strong and handsome," said Sir Desmond the Daring, "and I also have a proper hero-type name."

"All the others had proper hero-type names, and they turned out to be rubbish," said the boy. "I wanted to go to Hero School and learn how to fight monsters just like you did. But they just laughed and sent me to work in the ponkiest cheese shop in the kingdom."

"Why was that?" asked Sir Desmond.

"Because my name is Stinkpot," said the boy.

The crowd laughed.

"Don't you start," said Stinkpot.

"If you think you can save us all from the Monster, why don't you have a go?" said Sir Desmond.

"Steady on, Royal Hero!" whispered the King. "If the boy succeeds, he'll be His Majesty King Stinkpot the First! What kind of name is that for a king?"

"Don't worry, sire," said Sir Desmond with a wicked smile. "He doesn't stand a chance."

So they gave Stinkpot a sword, stuck him on a donkey and set him off to find the Monster.

In no time, Stinkpot found himself in a dark and scary forest. His donkey's teeth started to chatter with fear.

"Calm down," said Stinkpot, who was looking forward to being a hero at last. "I bet the monster isn't all *that* big and scary."

At that very moment, the ground began to shake and . . .

. . . the massive and menacing Monster burst
out of the trees in front of him.

"RRRRROOOOOOOOOOAAAAAAARRRRR!"
it roared, so loud that half the forest fell over.

"Oh plums!" gulped Stinkpot.

The Monster flashed its horns and gnashed its jaws. It crashed its spikes and clashed its claws. The pong from its terrible armpits was so revolting, Stinkpot's poor donkey fainted. But Stinkpot was used to horrible smells after all the time he'd spent in the cheese shop.

"You PUNY little WORM!" roared the Monster.
"I'm AMAZED anything so SMALL and WEEDY
would DARE to come after ME!"

All of a sudden Stinkpot wasn't scared any more. He was cross.

"How very rude!" he said. "Calling people names! Just because *you've* got a proper big and scary name, you think you're something special, is that it?"

"No!" roared the Monster.

"I bet you have got a scary name though!"
Stinkpot went on. "What is it? *The Crazy Castle
Crusher? The Dreaded Dungeon Demon?
The Knobbly Knight Nibbler?*"

"As a matter of fact, my name's. . ." said the
Monster, and then it mumbled something.

"Sorry," said Stinkpot, "I didn't hear that."

"I said. . ." said the Monster, and then it mumbled again.

"Louder, please," said Stinkpot.

"All right, all right!" snapped the Monster. "My name is. . ."

And the Monster took a deep breath, and in its scariest, rumbliest voice, it said:

"The what, sorry?" said Stinkpot.

"The Tickly-Wickly Poo-Poo Beast!" repeated the Monster crossly.

"Poo-Poo Beast?" said Stinkpot. "Really?"
And he started to laugh.

"Never mind what my name is!" roared the Monster angrily. "I'll gobble you up in one bite, don't you worry!"

"I'm sure you will," said Stinkpot. He should have been terrified, but he just couldn't stop laughing.

And then something odd happened.

A big fat tear appeared in one of the Monster's eyes and rolled all the way down its face.

And then another, and another.

The Monster was crying!

"Everyone in Monster School laughed at me because of my name," it sobbed, "and no one wanted to be my friend."

"That's not why I'm laughing," said Stinkpot.
"I'm laughing because my name is Stinkpot
Whiffington Honk!"

"Stinkpot Whiffington Honk?" said the Monster.
"What kind of name is THAT for a hero?"

"Exactly!" laughed Stinkpot.
And the Monster started laughing too.
They became best friends on the spot.
Then Stinkpot had an idea.

When Stinkpot returned to the castle, Sir Desmond the Daring laughed in his face.

"Ran away, did you, smelly trousers?" he said. "I can't say I'm surprised. Who ever heard of a hero called *Stinkpot*?"

"It is a very silly name, you're right," said
Stinkpot. "Almost as silly as The Tickly-Wickly
Poo-Poo Beast!"

"Now that *is* a silly name!" agreed Sir Desmond.

"Did somebody mention me?" said the Monster, suddenly rearing up right next to him.

"Eek!" shrieked Sir Desmond, and he stopped laughing at once. He was so scared that he ran off and hid . . .

. . . somewhere that made a dreadful mess of his armour.

And that's how Stinkpot became King Stinkpot the First.

On his very first day as king, he changed the law. Now people could do whatever job they wanted, no matter what they were called.

People called Baker could be butchers. People called Butcher could be bakers.

People called *The Daring* could work in the ponkiest cheese shop in the kingdom.

And you could be a Royal Hero, and defend the kingdom, even if your name was something really, really silly. . .

Like *The Tickly Wickly Poo-Poo Beast*!